Toestomper
and the Caterpillars

This book is dedicated to my grandchildren,
Alexandre and Laura Pederson.

Copyright © 1999 by Sharleen Collicott

All rights reserved. For information about permission
to reproduce selections from this book, write to
Permissions, Houghton Mifflin Company,
215 Park Avenue South, New York, New York 10003.

The text of this book is set in 16-point Cremona.
The illustrations are gouache, reproduced in full color.

Library of Congress Cataloging-in-Publication Data

Collicott, Sharleen.
Toestomper and the caterpillars / written and illustrated by Sharleen Collicott.
p.   cm.
Summary: Toestomper, who is mean, rude, and disgusting, changes his ways
after he destroys the home of a bunch of caterpillars and is forced to adopt
them.
ISBN 0-395-91168-0
[1. Caterpillars — Fiction. 2. Behavior — Fiction.]   I. Title.
PZ7.C67758To   1999
[Fic] — dc21   98-23268 CIP AC

Manufactured in the United States of America

WOZ 10 9 8 7 6 5 4 3 2

Toestomper
and the Caterpillars

Sharleen Collicott

Houghton Mifflin Company
Boston

Toestomper lived alone and liked it that way. But sometimes when he felt a little lonely, he would go to town and hang out with the Rowdy Ruffians.

"Hello, you lowlife rascals," he would greet them.

The Rowdy Ruffians liked Toestomper because Toestomper
was mean, rude . . .

. . . and disgusting.

One day when Toestomper went to town, his friends weren't there. Toestomper had to cause trouble all by himself. "This town is boring," he said, and he stomped out of town.

On his way home he saw a bunch of caterpillars in a bush. Toestomper stomped the bush flat and growled, "Don't sleep in a bush, you hairy crybabies. Build a hut like everyone else."

The caterpillars didn't know how to build a hut. They
followed Toestomper home to learn.

"Get away from me, you creepy creepers!" he shouted.

The caterpillars tried hard to build a hut by themselves, but
it fell over. They looked at Toestomper with tears in their eyes.
Their tiny tongues were dry.

Toestomper growled, "Here, you squishy wigglys, drink this
water. And now leave me alone!"

When the sun went down, the caterpillars shivered outside his door. Toestomper put a blanket in a box, and the caterpillars crawled inside to sleep.

"Don't get used to it," he warned. "This is only for one night."

Later that evening, the Rowdy Ruffians came over to play cards. Toestomper cheated, like he always did. "Those furry slugs are driving me crazy," he complained.

When Barfy talked about the mischief he had done that day, Toestomper didn't listen. "There must be fifty of those fuzzy bugs following me around," he growled.

"Can't you talk about anything except those stupid caterpillars?"
Nightmare asked.

Toestomper continued, "They can't even build a hut!"

Nightmare banged the table and shouted, "I'm leaving. I can't play cards with all this caterpillar talk." Then he poured lemonade over Toestomper.

"We're leaving too!" Basher and Barfy yelled.

As Toestomper's friends left, Basher kicked over the caterpillar box.

"Hey!" Toestomper shouted. "Be careful!"

The caterpillars sat close to Toestomper and made soft sounds. They tried to clean up the lemonade, but their little feet stuck to the floor.

"You hairy crawlers aren't good for much," said Toestomper, "but at least you don't dump food on me."

The next morning, Basher knocked on Toestomper's door.
"Let's go to town and be mean."
"I can't," Toestomper answered. "We're eating breakfast."

Then Nightmare stuck his head through the window.
"Let's go to town and be rude."

"Not today," said Toestomper. "We're reading a book."

A little later, Barfy walked by.
"Come on, Toestomper, let's go to town and be disgusting."

"Not now. I want to build a buggy."

"Toestomper isn't fun anymore," Basher whispered to
Nightmare. "All he cares about are those dumb caterpillars.
We have to do something about this."

The next day, the Rowdy Ruffians came by again.
"Come outside, Toestomper," Basher called.
When Toestomper opened the door, his friends yanked him
out, tied him up, and fastened him to a branch. Toestomper
yelled and cursed. He tried to stomp, but he couldn't move.

"We're taking the caterpillars," Barfy told him. "It's for your own good."

"Look out, hairballs!" Toestomper shouted. "Run and hide!"

Catching the caterpillars wasn't easy.

"Do we have them all?" Barfy asked.

"Absolutely," answered Nightmare. "Now let's go find the birds."

But Nightmare was wrong. A few of the caterpillars had got away.

The birds were eating lunch in a big oak tree.
"Would you like some dessert?" Nightmare asked.

"Yum yum," said the birds.

The frightened caterpillars heard *stomp stomp stomp* in the distance. Suddenly Toestomper was in the tree.

"DON'T EAT MY CATERPILLARS!" he shouted.

"Excuse us! So sorry!" said the birds. "We didn't know these desserts belonged to you."

Toestomper gathered up his caterpillars.

"Follow me, you frazzled fuzzies. Let's get your buggy. We're going to town."

Toestomper wheeled his caterpillars into a clothing store.

"Give me the smallest size you have," he said.

"Adorable," the townsfolk said. "Just delightful."

The Rowdy Ruffians laughed at Toestomper.

"Toestomper is a sissy," they jeered. "He hangs out with little dressed-up bugs."

"These are my new friends," Toestomper said in a proud voice that startled the Rowdy Ruffians.

"Climb into your buggy, my fancy dandies," he said.

Then Toestomper took his caterpillars home and built them their own hut.

From then on, Toestomper was very busy.

He hardly ever had time to be mean, rude, or disgusting.

And he was never lonely.

Once in a while they let the Rowdy Ruffians come over to play cards.

Toestomper and the caterpillars always won.